To Pam and Martin,

who made me get on with it.

Hug Me is © Flying Eye Books 2014.

This is a fifth edition.

First published in 2014 by Flying Eye Books, an imprint of Nobrow Ltd.
27 Westgate Street, London E8 3RL

Text and Illustrations © Simona Ciraolo 2014.
Simona Ciraolo has asserted her right under the Copyright, Designs and
Patents Act, 1988, to be identified as the Author and Illustrator of this Work.

Published in the US by Nobrow (US) Inc.
Printed in Latvia on FSC® certified paper.

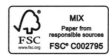

FSC
www.fsc.org

MIX
Paper from
responsible sources
FSC® C002795

ISBN: 978-1-909263-49-9
Order from www.flyingeyebooks.com

Simona Ciraolo

Hug me

Felipe

FLYING EYE BOOKS

LONDON - NEW YORK

Felipe was descended from an old and famous
family who liked to look good and
always behaved properly.

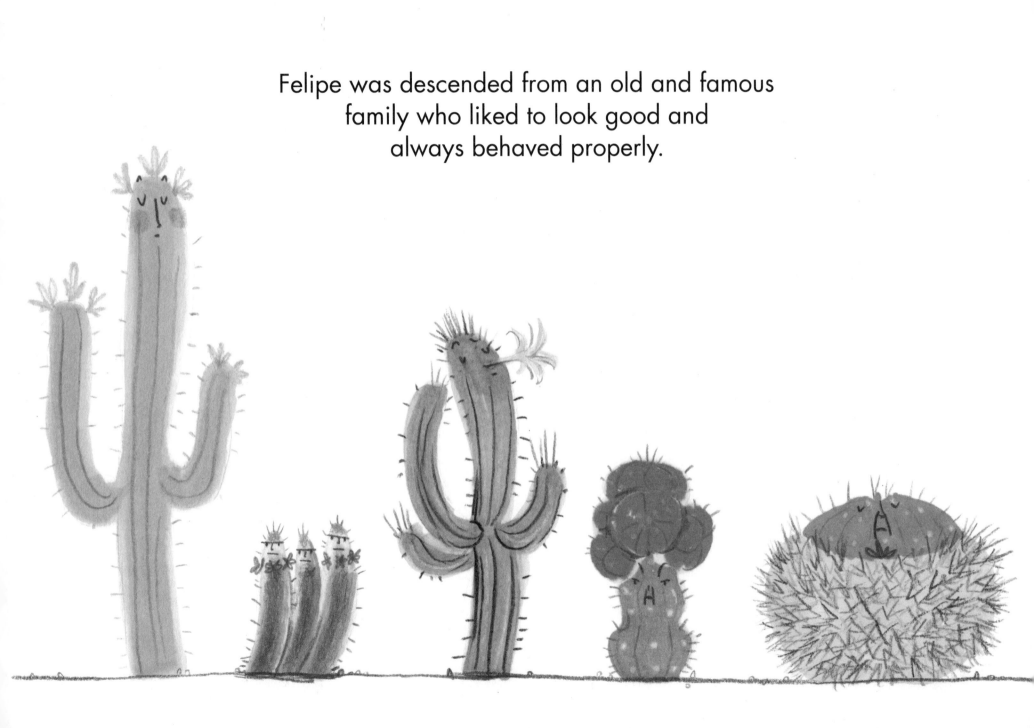

His family kept everything neat and tidy and they
believed one should never trespass into
another's personal space.

Felipe was taught
to keep still,

encouraged to be looked at

and told that one day
he'd reach a high position.

But Felipe thought his family worried about all the wrong things.

They didn't notice that all he wanted was a hug.

Of course, he could see
his family wasn't the
touchy feely type,

so he wished
someone else

would come and
put their arms
around him,

but no one ever did.

One day, Felipe made a new acquaintance.

He was bold, confident

and he was trouble.

But Felipe couldn't see that,

and they grew closer and closer,

until the day
disaster struck...

Felipe was blamed and made to feel very bad.

No one in his family thought of
giving him a hug.

Clearly,
he didn't
belong there.

For a while Felipe hoped
he would find a new family,

but wherever he went,
he wasn't welcome.

So he learned to enjoy his own company and thought he didn't need anyone else after all.

During all this time
Felipe felt very lonely.

But what he didn't know was…

someone else was feeling lonely too.

The day he realized that...

Felipe knew just what to do.

MAR 2019
(2014)